FRIENDSHIP'S FIRST THANKSGIVING

written and illustrated by
WILLIAM ACCORSI

Holiday House / New York

Library of Congress Cataloging-in-Publication Data
Accorsi, William.
Friendship's first Thanksgiving / written and illustrated by
William Accorsi.
p.   cm.
Summary: Friendship, a dog who has crossed the sea with the
Pilgrims, describes the colony's first year in the New World,
culminating in the first Thanksgiving feast.
ISBN 0-8234-0963-5
[1. Pilgrims, (New Plymouth Colony)—Fiction.   2. Thanksgiving Day—
Fiction.   3. Dogs—Fiction.]   I. Title.
PZ7.A173Fr   1992   91–45132   CIP   AC
[E]—dc20

For Dolly Dingle, Zazu, Kiddo, and the
princess of Piqua, Ohio, Caroline Pool

My name is Friendship. I traveled to the New World with the Pilgrims on the *Mayflower*. This is my story.

We sailed from England, leaving many friends and relatives behind. After a number of days at sea, the winter storms came. Strong winds howled loudly and huge waves tumbled across the deck. We became wet and cold and prayed that the ship would not sink. After we had been sailing for many weeks, a sailor high up on the mast called out, "Land ho!"

Everyone cheered. "Land ho! Land ho!" they all cried.
"We made it. We will be landing soon!"

I ran around the ship barking, "Arf, arf, land ho!—arf,
arf, land ho!"

The *Mayflower* anchored off the coast. We knew very little about this new land. We didn't know if the Indians were friendly and if we'd find fierce wild animals such as wolves and bears.

Our leaders decided to send some men ashore. We reached dry land and knelt, giving thanks to God for our safe journey across the sea. We walked several miles. We didn't see any Indians or fierce wild animals. We rowed back to the *Mayflower* before dark.

We made several trips in the small boat, searching for a good place to live. On one trip we were excited to see six Indians and an Indian dog on the beach. They saw us, too, and ran into the woods. We ran after them. We wanted to make friends.

I barked after the Indian dog. The dog barked back. The Indians had disappeared. I was disappointed that I was not able to make friends with the Indian dog.

After several days of exploring, we found a nice place to live. It had a good harbor deep enough for ships, a hill where we could build a fort, and many springs with fresh, clean water. The soil was good for farming.

Now the days were getting colder. We began to build our houses. We cut trees and sawed them into lumber. We gathered tall grass and leafy branches to thatch the roofs.

I was not too good at building houses. I looked after the youngest children and watched out for Indians and wild animals. I also went hunting with the men. I was good at chasing rabbits and finding game birds.

One day, I went into the woods to gather thatch with my Pilgrim master. We had worked for several hours when we heard the howling of wolves. They were close by. My master broke off a large stick from a tree to use as a weapon.

The wolves circled us for a long time. I was worried. I think the wolves were interested in eating me. I was so skinny, I doubt I would have tasted very good. Maybe the wolves changed their minds about me because they finally left to look for a better meal.

The winter grew dreadfully cold. There was a shortage of food and many of our people became ill and died. Although we could not see any Indians, we knew they were watching us. We buried our dead friends at night so the Indians could not see how many had died.

The good captain of the *Mayflower* stayed on his ship in the harbor during the long winter. He would not return to England until he felt we no longer needed his help. With the Lord watching over us, we made it through the coldest months.

One day, as I was watching for wild animals, a tall Indian came out of the woods. He walked straight toward our houses. He held up his hand and said, "Welcome Englishman." I ran alongside him, barking loudly. I pretended I found this Indian all by myself and was taking him to meet our people.

Our visiting Indian was called Samoset. He spoke some of our language. He told us about an Indian named Squanto who had met many white men and could also speak our language. Several days later, we met Squanto. He became our good friend and helper.

When spring came, he taught us how to fish, hunt, and gather seafood. He helped us plant our corn. He showed us how to dig a hole and place a fish in the soil with corn seed to make the corn grow. My job was to watch for wild animals. We did not want them to dig up the fish.

It was now time for the captain of the *Mayflower* and his crew to go back to England. We were sad to see the ship sail away.

The days were getting much warmer. It was wonderful to enjoy summer. And food! There was so much to eat. We remembered how little food there had been in the past few months. We worked all summer preparing for the coming winter. Everyone helped, even the small children. They gathered nuts, berries, and dry twigs for our cooking fires. When autumn came, we harvested our crops and gave thanks to the Lord for his blessings and to our Indian friends for their help. We invited the Indians to a Thanksgiving feast.

It was exciting to see the Indians dressed in their finest clothing. They brought food to share with us. Best of all, the Indian dog we had seen many months before also came.

She and I had a wonderful visit. The Pilgrims and the Indians spoke different languages, but my friend and I spoke the same dog language. I explained that my name is Friendship because I am man's best friend. She said her Indian name is Caniscoot, which means "fast-running dog" and that the Indians also considered her their best friend. Caniscoot gave me a turkey feather. I gave her my favorite bone that I had brought from England.

It was a glorious Thanksgiving. There were games and shooting contests. The Indians danced and told stories. Finally, after three days of celebration, the bonfires died down.

Tired and full, I fell asleep by the glowing embers
with Caniscoot. This was the beginning of our long
friendship.

NOTES ON THE ILLUSTRATIONS

I am not an artist who practices "realism." In my sculpture and art-work, I have made use of that wonderful resource called *artistic license.* Thus the graphic representations of the Indians and other characters in this book are stylized rather than literally accurate.

NOTES ON THE STORY

Europeans had been sailing the waters off North America for almost one hundred years before the Pilgrims landed. They traded with the coastal Indians for food and furs. Thousands of Indians caught dis-eases from the Europeans and died.

A few years before the Pilgrims landed, Squanto had been taken aboard a European ship and sold in Spain as a slave. He eventually returned home on another European ship, only to discover that all his people had perished of a white man's disease.

★ ★ ★

Contrary to popular belief, the Pilgrims did own and wear colorful clothing!

★ ★ ★

The Pilgrims were introduced to popcorn at the first Thanksgiving.

At the next Thanksgiving, Friendship and Caniscoot brought their six puppies. Three were given Indian names, "Chase the Bird," "Chase the Rabbit," and "Chase His Own Tail." The other three were given white people's names, "Pal," "Spit," and "Rover."

William Accorsi
March 15, 1992